Nature Trail

Alison Hawes
Illustrated by Rosalind Beardshaw

We like this little snail.

We like this little slug.

We like this little worm.

We like this little bug.

We like this little frog.

We like this little mouse.

We like little animals . . .

but not in this house!